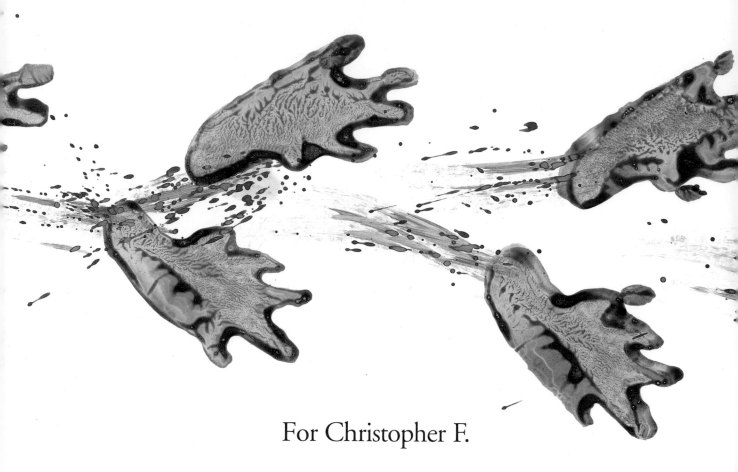

# For Christopher F.

A Red Fox Book

Published by Random House Children's Books 20 Vauxhall Bridge Road, London SW1V 2SA

A division of Random House UK Ltd
London Melbourne Sydney Auckland Johannesburg and agencies throughout the world

Copyright © Ruth Brown  1996

1 3 5 7 9 10 8 6 4 2

First published in Great Britain by Andersen Press Ltd 1996

Red Fox edition 1999

Printed in Hong Kong

RANDOM HOUSE UK Limited Reg. No. 954009

ISBN 0 09 940382 X

# TOAD

# Ruth Brown

RED FOX

This is the tale of a monstrous toad,

a muddy toad, a slimy toad,
a clammy, sticky, gooey toad,

odorous, stinking, filthy and foul,
and smelling of stagnant water.

He's covered in warts and lumps and bumps,
stained and soiled, spotted and speckled,

poisonous, septic, toxic and bitter,
and oozing venomous fluids.

The monstrous toad is a greedy toad, a
fly-munching, bug-crunching, worm-slurping toad.

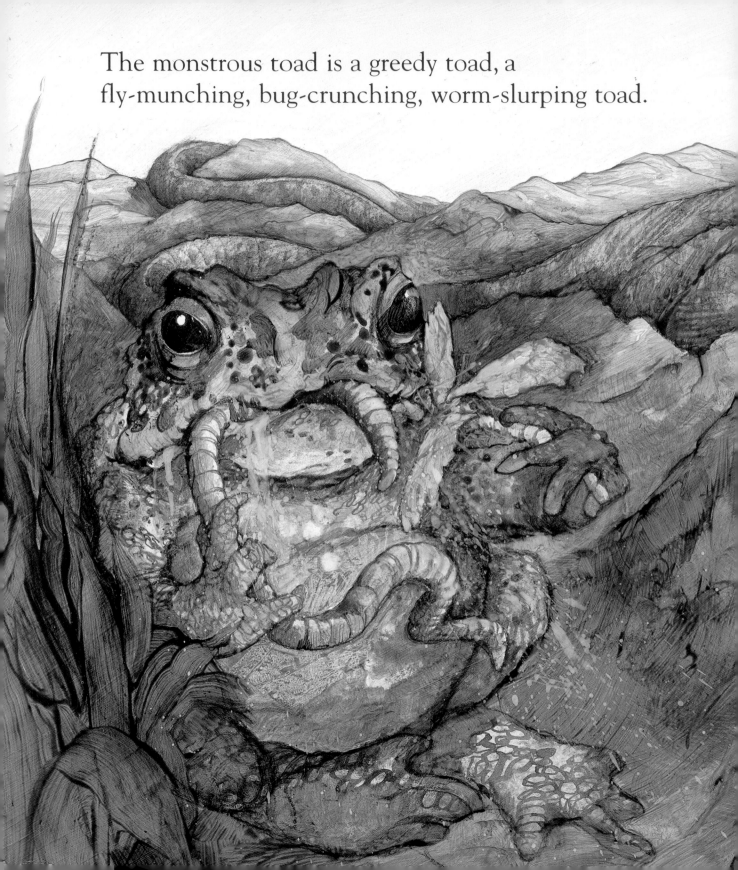

He is clumsy, careless, short-sighted and slow,

and he waddles and stumbles,
winking and blinking,

straight into the jaws of a monster!

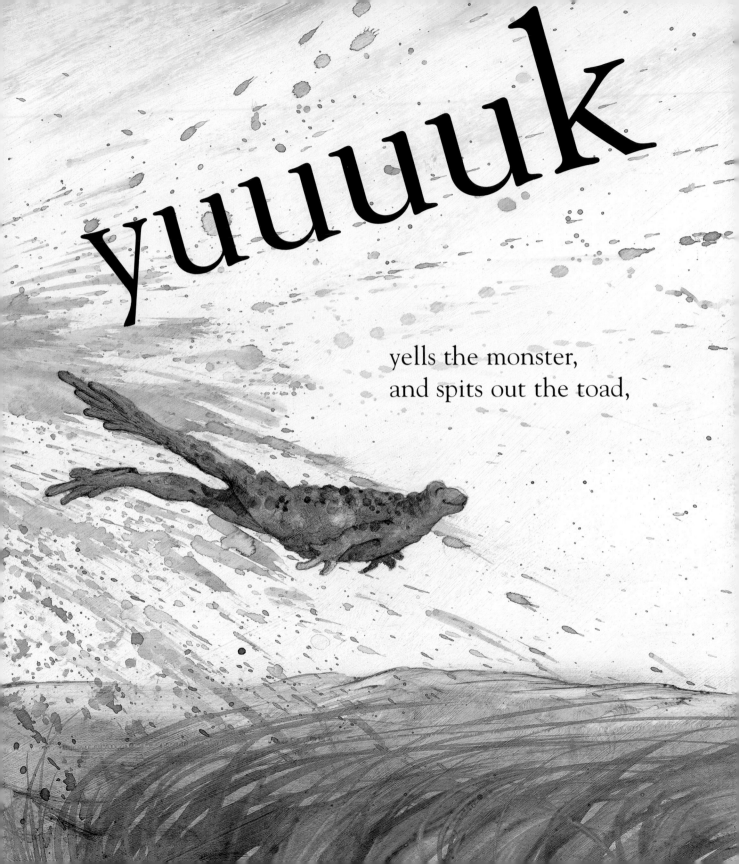

# yuuuuk

yells the monster,
and spits out the toad,

the happy toad, the carefree toad,
the safe, secure, self-confident toad,

who smiles a monstrous smile.

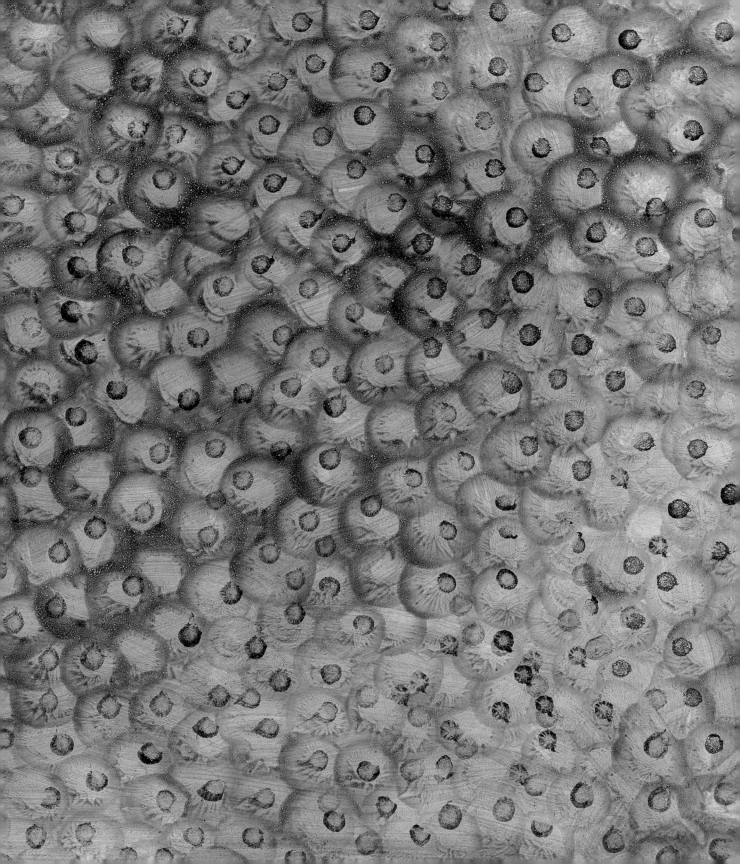